The
Adventures
of
Willie

The Adventures of Willie

Dorothy Clewes

Illustrated by
Caroline Crossland

Julia MacRae Books

LONDON SYDNEY AUCKLAND JOHANNESBURG

Upsidedown Willie copyright © 1968 Dorothy Clewes
Special Branch Willie copyright © 1969 Dorothy Clewes
Fire-Brigade Willie copyright © 1970 Dorothy Clewes
Copyright in this collected edition
The Adventures of Willie © 1991 Dorothy Clewes
Illustrations copyright © 1991 Caroline Crossland
All rights reserved
Upsidedown Willie, *Special Branch Willie* and *Fire Brigade Willie*
were all originally published in Great Britain 1968, 1969 and 1970
respectively by Hamish Hamilton (Gazelle Books)
The Adventures of Willie first published in Great Britain 1991
by Julia MacRae Books
A division of Random Century Ltd
20, Vauxhall Bridge Road, London SW1V 2SA

Random Century Australia (Pty) Ltd
20 Alfred Street, Milsons Point, Sydney, NSW 2061

Random Century New Zealand Ltd
PO BOX 40 – 086, Glenfield, Auckland 10, New Zealand

Random Century South Africa (Pty) Ltd
PO BOX 337, Bergvlei, 2021, South Africa

Printed and bound in Great Britain by
Butler & Tanner Ltd, Frome and London

British Library Cataloguing in Publication Data
Clewes, Dorothy
The Adventures of Willie
I. Title II. Crossland, Caroline
023. 914
ISBN 1–85681–091–7

CONTENTS

Upsidedown Willie

Willie had just learned to stand on his head. Yesterday he had wobbled about but today he was as steady as if he had been born that way.

"Look, Mum, I can do it." He had practised for days and at last he had mastered it.

"So you can," his mother said, absently, seeing him out of the corner of her eye, busy with the baking.

"No, Mum, you're not really looking."

His mother lifted her floury hands out of the basin and turned and looked at Willie, feet in the air, his hands where his feet ought to be, his face very red, his hair dusting the kitchen floor. "Silly boy," she said, "you'll turn your brain."

Willie flopped back on his feet. The room spun round and then came to a standstill. "My brain didn't turn but the room did," he said.

"Boys," his mother said, – "whatever will you think of

next?" – and was very glad that the new baby had turned out to be a girl.

"What are you making?" Willie asked his mother, rightsideup now and bored, wondering what to do.

"Sausage rolls, and little cakes for tea," his mother said.

"Can I have one?" Willie asked.

"They're not even cooked yet."

Willie stood watching his mother as she rolled the long snake of sausage meat up in its cover of pastry and cut it into neat little wedges, and then he was bored with that. He went out of the back door and into the garden and stopped for a moment to look at the new baby, snug and fast asleep in its pram. It wasn't good for anything yet, wrapped up just like a sausage in its blankets, but as soon as it could walk he would teach it to stand on its head. He would teach it a lot of other things, too, and then it wouldn't be so bad, but babies took such a long time to grow.

He kicked his way round the garden and then went off into the street. He wished there was someone he could show off to. And presently there was. Coming towards him down the street was the postman. The postman was an old friend of Willie's. Often he would stop and speak to him – as he did now.

"Haven't seen you lately. Thought you must have started school."

Willie shook his head. He wished he was old enough to go to school, but that wouldn't be until the end of the year. "I've been teaching myself, though. Watch," – and he leaned forward, put both hands flat down on the pavement, gave a little spring and there he was, upsidedown and straight as a lamp-post.

The postman looked at upsidedown Willie in amazement.

"That's good," he said. "That's very good, that is."

"I can stay like it for hours," Willie said. He meant seconds, really, but when you are upsidedown time goes much slower and seconds seem like hours.

"I don't ever remember being able to do that," the postman said. "You ought to be in a circus."

Willie came rightsideup again, his red face beaming delightedly. "Do you think so?"

"I certainly do," the postman said. "Anyone who can stand on their head for hours is wasted feetontheground."

It would be fun, working in a circus, Willie thought. He'd be as good as the man on the high wire, and the man on stilts. He'd be the Upsidedown Man and his name would be written up in big letters on the posters outside. "I'll think about it," Willie said.

He walked back with the postman as far as where he lived and then went in again to see if the sausage rolls and the little cakes were cooked yet.

His mother was just taking them out of the oven. "They're red hot, you'll burn your mouth," she said as Willie stretched out a hand and helped himself. He blew on the sausage roll until it was cool enough to eat and then he stood on his head again.

"Stop standing on your head and do something useful," his mother said. She was tired of seeing Willie with his feet where his head should be.

When the milkman came rattling up the garden path Willie was standing upsidedown by the kitchen door. He had only just got himself up in that position but it looked as if he had been standing there forever.

"You gave me a start," the milkman said. "I thought you were a suit of clothes hanging up to dry. I thought your mother must have forgotten to take you out before she washed them."

Willie turned himself rightwayup. "When I'm standing on my head you look upsidedown," he told the milkman, and added: "As a matter of fact, I'm training to be in a circus."

He hadn't known he was going to say that but when the words came tumbling out he knew they must have been there, waiting, ever since the postman had spoken them.

"You are?" the milkman echoed. "It wouldn't be the one that's coming into town next week, would it?" he added, jokingly.

Willie hadn't known anything about any circus coming into town but the postman must have known, that was why he'd mentioned it. Postmen knew everything: who people were and often what they did, but mostly where they lived. Tomorrow he would ask him where the circus was going to be. He said now to the milkman: "Of course, that's why I'm practising."

He waited for the postman next morning, standing upsidedown by the front gate. A dog came up and licked his forehead enquiringly, thinking he must be some new kind of animal and Willie had to make a big shout before he would go away. But at last the postman turned the corner of Willie's street – two big booted feet first, long black-trousered legs next, and then the rest of him. He hadn't any letters for Willie's address but he stopped to speak just the same. "Upsidedown Willie, that's what I'm going to call you," he

said. "Have you been like that ever since I saw you
yesterday?"

"Not all the time, but mostly," Willie said, coming
rightsideup because that way it was easier to talk. "Where's

the circus going to be – the one that's coming to town next week?"

"Oh – so you know all about it," the postman said. "Now, let me think–" and a deep, thinking look came on his face. It cleared in a moment and he said: "On the Waste, back of the dairy."

Of course, Willie thought, that was why the milkman had known all about it. He ought to have known about it himself because he often went to play on the Waste. He knew that it wasn't going to be waste-ground for much longer because a high block of offices was planned to go up there. In the meantime anyone could use it.

"Don't tell me, let me guess," the postman said. "You're going to join them and you'll be the star attraction, I shouldn't be surprised,"– and he went off down the road, chuckling.

"Willie, go and fetch my shoes from the menders," his mother called from the house, " – and don't cross the road without the policeman." She also hoped he would take his time about it and not walk there on his hands instead of his feet.

There was always a policeman on this crossing. When he saw Willie standing on the edge of the pavement he put up a hand and all the cars and bicycles and buses stopped. Willie felt very important walking across to the other side of the road while all the traffic waited. It must feel very grand, he thought, being able to stop traffic like that. For a little while after he had reached the other side, he stood and watched the policeman directing it first this way and then the other, and then he walked on.

Willie collected the shoes. He carried them carefully so as not to spoil the two little black silk bows that decorated them. When he came to the crossing the policeman held up the traffic again. Willie wished he could have walked over on his hands but walking upsidedown was a lot more difficult than just standing upsidedown. He'd got to be perfect at that before he learned anything else.

When he got home he handed the shoes to his mother and then went up to his bedroom.

All that week Willie practised in his room, every day. He stood on his head in the morning, in the afternoon, and in the evening before he got into bed, so that his mother said to his father:

"I'm worried about Willie, all that standing on his head.

Every time I look at him he's wrong way up. It can't be good for him."

"I stood on my head when I was his age," his father said, not at all worried. "He'll get tired of it soon enough, you'll see."

"Then I suppose it will be cartwheels," his mother sighed. In her mind she could see Willie, wheeling like a hoop in one room and out of another. She hoped he would get tired of it before the new baby decided to copy him, girl or no girl.

Willie saw the circus come into town. It was really a very small one, on its way to join up with a larger one outside a big city. Here and there on their way they stopped a night or two and put on a performance. The money they took helped to pay the travelling expenses. It wasn't a rich circus. They could do with every penny.

First came a string of caravans, chrome shining like silver, curtains at the tiny windows. Then a few ponies ridden by boys and girls who did not look very much older than Willie himself, and after them came two trailers. Willie, along with a lot of other children from the town, followed the caravans until they got to the Waste. The caravans and the trailers bumped their way over the broken pavement and up on to the rough, neglected ground. The ponies picked their way more carefully, stepping aside from the pot-holes and the bricks and the rubble. Willie watched them for a long time, long after the other children had got tired and moved away.

He watched while the trailers were emptied and while the roundabouts were fixed and tested. He watched while the Big Top went up and the canvas walls came down round it to make a proper little theatre. He stayed there so long that at last one of the men spoke to him:

"Isn't it time you went home, sonny?"

"I want to join the circus," Willie said.

"Oh, you do, do you?" the man said. "What do you think you can do?"

"I can stand on my head," Willie said, "like this –" and he leaned forward, put both hands flat on the ground, gave a little spring and there he was, upsidedown and straight as the pole that held up the Big Top.

"Not bad," the man said. "Not bad at all."

"Can I stand on my head in the circus, then?" Willie asked him.

"Come back tomorrow," the man said. "Right now we're too busy to think straight." He'd never met a boy yet who didn't want to join them. They stood around watching while the circus was set up and imagined themselves walking the High Wire, riding the ponies, playing clown – until it got to lunch-time or tea-time or supper-time, and then they went home and forgot all about it.

Willie went home but he did not forget about it. He went to bed early and practised harder than ever. He could now do things like eating upsidedown, which meant balancing on one hand for a moment or two while he popped pieces of biscuit into his mouth. He tried drinking water that way, too, but it came down his nose and made him sneeze.

"Now he's caught a cold," he heard his mother say to his father, "– and not to be wondered at, walking about on hands instead of on well-shod feet."

Willie could not get to the Waste quickly enough next

morning. Now it looked like a real circus, the caravans circling the pitch, side-shows and shooting-galleries and coconut shies spread around, and in the middle of it all and taking up most of the space, was the Big Top. There was a lovely smell, too – of horses, and sawdust, and hot oil, and smoke from the outdoor cooking stoves. Willie followed the cooking smell round to the back of the Big Top and there were the circus people, the boys and girls who had ridden the ponies, the men who had driven the caravans and the trailers – and the man who yesterday had said: "Come back tomorrow."

The man was sitting on an upturned orange box, a mug of tea in one hand and a large piece of bread and cheese in the other. He wasn't too busy to think now, and when he saw Willie the thought popped into his head

that just now and again you came across a boy who really

believed that you meant all you said.

"Did I say that?" he said, knowing very well that he had but wanting to give himself time to think up an answer.

"You said: Not bad at all, come back tomorrow," Willie replied, and stood upsidedown to remind him.

This time he had an audience and at once a little round of applause and cheering broke out.

"He's good," one said.

"As good as any of you," one of the grown-ups called across to the boys and girls.

" – and a lot younger," another said.

"What else can you do?" the man asked him.

Willie came rightsideup again. He hadn't thought he would have to do anything else.

"I mean – could you do it on the High Wire? Or on horseback?" the man said. He knew Willie wouldn't be able to but it was kinder, he felt, to let Willie see for himself that he wasn't good enough for a circus.

"I can do it on one hand – but not for long," Willie said. He decided not to mention the eating or the drinking as neither had been a great success. He looked hopefully at the man and now the man had already got his mouth open to say

No when one of the young people at the back called out:

"Let him hand out tickets at the tent – upsidedown."

"That's right," another called. "The Show that starts before you get inside."

"– and him being a little 'un," a big woman said, "he'd be a draw, that's what he'd be."

"All right," the man said, remembering how he had felt when he had landed his first job. "Can't pay much, mind you, but it'll keep you in ice-cream."

Willie could not believe it. He was part of the circus. Upsidedown Willie taking tickets at the entrance to the Big Top, just as the postman said.

"A mug of tea and a slice of bread and cheese for the young 'un," the man called, and Willie went to sit down among them all.

"What's your ma going to say?" the big woman asked him.

"She told me to go and do something useful," Willie said. He didn't think this was what she had had in mind exactly, but he was quite sure she would be glad for him to be out of the way for a bit.

"Time to get ready," the man said.

When they were all dressed up they looked quite different.

The girls were dressed in tights and spangled bodices, with feathers and jewels in their hair. The boys were in tights, too, with satin shirts and buckles on their shoes. The clowns

had painted faces so that Willie did not recognise them at all. The man who seemed to be the boss now wore a black, flowing cloak and a silk top hat and he carried a long, cracking whip in his hand. Willie was given a special clown suit to put on.

"Hey, Upsidedown Willie," the big woman called. "Your job is at the entrance with me." She was sitting at a small table by the tent flap, a tin to hold the takings beside her and a box full of tickets which she was now putting down on the ground beside her and in front of Willie.

Willie had not stopped to think that his part in the circus was outside the Big Top and not inside where all the fun was going on. He hesitated only a moment, though, and then obediently tipped himself up to stand by the table.

"Walk up! Walk up!" the big woman cried. "Take your tickets from Upsidedown Willie and see the Big Show inside. Born standing on his head," she cried. "What you do on your feet Willie does on his head. Walk up! Walk up!"

And people began walking up: big boots, little boots, shoes and slippers, sandals and Wellingtons, stockings and socks, because that was all Willie could see of the customers. He would not have been able to tell you what else they wore, he could only guess from what the big woman was crying out:

"Two for the gentleman in the blue shirt," she would shout, and "Three for the lady in the yellow jumper," and "Four for the soldier with medals on his chest."

No soldier could have stood stiffer to attention than Willie, balancing on one hand while he handed up the tickets and hoped they would not come more than four at a time because that was as long as he could balance on one hand without toppling over.

When all the customers had gone inside Willie was allowed to take a rest rightsideup, but he wasn't allowed to slip inside the tent in case a late customer should come and then he had to be ready to stand on his head again. He was beginning to feel tired. He wouldn't have noticed it so much but he could hear all that was going on inside the Big Top; the cracking of the whip, the thudding of the hooves of the horses, and the roars of delight from the customers who were watching all the fun he was missing.

There was a break for lunch and then it all began again.

"Walk up! Walk up! Take your tickets from Upsidedown Willie and see the Big Show inside. Born standing on his head. What you do on your feet Willie does on his hands. Walk up! Walk up!"

"Born standing on his head, did you hear that?" one woman said to another. "Poor little fellow. You don't know when you're lucky, do you?"

"One for a lady with black silk bows on her shoes," the big woman cried.

Willie recognised the shoes at once. They were black and shiny and had little black silk bows on them. They were the same shoes he had carried home from the menders only the day before.

"Willie! Stand up! At once!"

Willie was so thankful to be told to stand up that he did not mind at all that his mother's voice sounded angry. Angry, but at the same time, relieved. He came rightsideup and stood there, waiting.

When he had been ten minutes late for lunch instead of ten minutes too early for it, Willie's mother had not really worried. When he was half an hour late and then an hour she had wheeled the new baby round to her neighbour's and gone off to the police station to ask them to help her.

They had been very kind, had calmed her down with a cup of tea, and then had asked her lots of questions, and it had surprised her how easily they had arrived at the right answer. "We'll run you down to the circus right away," the Sergeant had said. "My bet is that you'll find him there," – and he was right.

"Willie – how could you?" Willie's mother did not care that everyone was staring at her, shaking Willie and hugging him by turns.

"He was only making himself useful – like you told him to," the big woman said. "Doing very nicely he was, too. A clever boy, that one. You should be proud of him." She dipped a hand into the box of money on her table. "Here," she said to Willie, "that's for doing your best."

The Sergeant had a soft spot for circuses and for circus people and so he did not say any of the things he might have said. He also knew what boys were like because he had been one himself, a long time ago. He could remember a time, actually, when he had wanted to join a circus but he hadn't managed to get into one as Willie had done. He was also a family man, and he knew how Willie's mother was feeling.

Willie gave back his clown suit. As they got into the car the policeman said: "Circuses are all right for kids, but you're a smart boy. You ought to be in the police force."

"Do you think so?" Willie was remembering the policeman who had directed the traffic at the crossing, making it do whatever he wanted it to do. Now, sitting alongside the Sergeant, he watched him. Every so often he would make the siren shrill out, and traffic and pedestrians would scuttle out of the way, pulling in to the side of the road as the car sped back to Willie's home. Willie thought how very important the Sergeant looked in his smart uniform: silver buttons shining, the silver chain that held his whistle hanging from his breast-pocket. It might be fun to be a policeman.

"I'll think about it," Willie said.

Special Branch Willie

PUBLISHER'S NOTE
The rules have changed since this story was first written and readers thinking about joining the Police Force might like to know that there are no longer any height restrictions.

Willie was standing in front of the dressing-table mirror in his bedroom. He was standing very straight, feet together, shoulders back, head up, chin tucked in. His reflection looked back at him, not smiling, very solemn. After a moment he raised his right arm as high as it would reach above his head and brought up his left arm straight and level with his shoulders.

"Willie!" his mother called from downstairs, "breakfast's ready."

Willie lowered his arms reluctantly. It was always the same, whenever he was busy it was either time for breakfast or time for dinner, time for tea or time for bed.

"What's the matter with you?" Willie's mother asked him. "You look as if you've swallowed the poker."

"I'm practising to be a policeman," Willie told her.

"Oh, I should have guessed."

Willie was always being something. The last time it had been a circus act, standing on his head more often than he was standing on his feet. If he was now going to be a policeman, at least he would be rightsideup.

"You've got a bit of growing to do first," his father told him.

"He's doing that fast enough." To his mother it seemed that she was always buying new shoes, new clothes, nothing was worn out before Willie needed a larger size.

Willie drew his spoon through his porridge to make a cross-roads. In the middle of the little square it made, he put a porridge-blob policeman.

"Willie!" his mother scolded him, "– eat up your porridge properly and stop playing games with it."

Willie broke up the porridge pavements with his spoon and drowned the policeman in a puddle of milk.

"Well, mind what you're up to," his father said. "Don't arrest anyone before I get home and don't upset the traffic in the High Street." He dived a hand into his pocket. "I don't know if policemen eat sweets but if they do here's twenty pence to buy some."

Willie put the money safely away in his pocket. Usually when he had money given to him he couldn't wait to get down to the Corner Sweet Shop to spend it – but at the moment there was something he wanted more than sweets, and that was a silver whistle on a chain. All policemen wore them, the silver chain threaded through a button-hole in their jacket and the whistle on the end of it tucked into a pocket. He hadn't quite enough money for it yet but the twenty pence brought the whistle a lot nearer.

The new baby was crawling across the hearth-rug. Willie held up the traffic while she got safely over and until she had disappeared under the table, then he ran round the table in time to stop her crawling out the other side. Surprised and frustrated, the baby set up a howl of protest. "Willie – stop teasing," his mother reproved him.

"I'm not teasing," Willie objected. "I'm teaching her road safety. She was coming out on to the main road without looking both ways. I'm holding her up until the lights change."

"Oh, for heaven's sake –" His mother sighed and whipped the baby up from underneath Willie's solidly planted-apart feet. "Go and play policemen in the garden," she told him. "There's plenty of room there and you won't be in anyone's way."

To get to the garden Willie had to pass through the hall. On the hall table, a note pad and pencil by its side, was the telephone. Willie put a finger inside the last little hole but one and dialled three times: 999. If you did it properly, lifting the handpiece off its rest, holding it to your ear, a voice would speak and ask if you wanted Fire, Police or Ambulance.

Willie had never actually heard the voice because he was never allowed to pick up the handpiece, but he dreamed about doing it, one day.

"Willie–" his mother called, as she always did, "how often do I have to tell you to leave the telephone alone?"

"I'm not telephoning properly, I'm only pretending," Willie called back.

"The telephone isn't for pretending games," his mother said, "it's for serious messages. Now – run along, do."

There was plenty of room in the garden as his mother had said, and no one to get in the way of – but if you were a policeman you needed something – or someone – in your way. Willie went and stood at the gate. There was one pedestrian coming down the road. He had a sack slung over his shoulder and a bundle of letters in one hand. It was the postman.

Willie strode out into the middle of the pavement and held up his right hand. The postman stopped obediently and let the imaginary lorry and half-a-dozen cars cross in front of him.

Willie lowered his arm, turned, and waved the postman on. "I'm practising to be a policeman," he told the postman.

"And a very good job you're making of it," the postman said. "If you hadn't been there I might have been run over."

Willie was delighted that the postman had taken him seriously instead of laughing at him and telling him to get out of the way. "You ought to be in the police force. They could do with smart boys like you," the postman said. "Of course, you'll have to grow a bit first."

And *that* was what his father had said, and of course it was true. To be a policeman you had to be tall enough and strong enough to handle dangerous criminals as well as traffic and pedestrians.

"Well, keep at it," the postman said encouragingly.

Willie heard the milkman's trolley before he saw it. He ran down the road and was there in time to wave him round the corner.

"I always did think there should be a policeman on that corner," the milkman said.

"I'm not a real policeman, yet," Willie told him. "I'm not tall enough or strong enough."

"Milk, that's the answer," the milkman said. "A pinta day: don't you watch the telly?"

Willie wasn't sure how much a pint was. He had milk for breakfast, he had it on his porridge, sometimes there was a milk pudding for dinner, and he had it again for tea – although often he did not drink it all because he did not like milk as much as all that.

"That's it, then," the milkman said, "you're not drinking enough of it."

When it came to dinner-time Willie held out his plate for a

second helping of rice pudding.

His mother was pleased. "I thought you didn't like milk puddings," she said.

At tea-time he drank up his milk to the very last drop.

"My goodness, what's come over you?" his mother said. "Yesterday I couldn't get it down you, today I can't give you enough."

"Have I had as much as a pint?" Willie asked her.

"Nearer two, I'd say," his mother said.

Willie wandered out into the garden. The baby was sleeping in its pram close by the kitchen door. "Can I push her around?" Willie asked. He could pretend the pram was a police car and that they were racing to the scene of a crime.

"No," his mother said, "– and don't make a noise or you'll wake her up. It will be bedtime soon, don't go too far away."

Willie went and stood at the gate, feet apart, hands clasped behind his back as he had seen policemen stand, but he soon got tired of that and in a moment started to walk down the street with slow, measured steps. At the end of the street there was a zebra crossing that took you over the road to the High Street. Willie stood by it watching the cars and the lorries and the bicycles whizz across. Once a car stopped, thinking Willie was waiting to get over to the other side. He waved it on and the car obeyed him. That's what happened when you were a policeman, people obeyed you. When the next car stopped for him to cross the road, Willie decided that he might as well. After all, the police station was on the other side and that was where he had been planning to go ever since he had decided to be a policeman.

The sergeant was standing behind his desk, smart in his blue uniform, the silver chain that held the whistle running down from his jacket buttonhole into his pocket, silver buttons shining. "What can I do for you?" he asked Willie.

"I want to be a policeman."

The sergeant looked Willie up and down. "You're a bit on the small side," he said. "Required height: five foot eight inches." The last time Willie was measured he had only been three foot and a bit. "Oh, you'll grow," the sergeant assured him, "– and when you do, come back and see us again."

Willie walked slowly back to the zebra crossing. It was going to be a long time before he could be a policeman. He stuffed his hands into his pockets and his fingers touched the twenty pence. And it was going to take for ever to save up for the silver whistle. He might as well go and spend it on sweets at the Corner Sweet Shop.

Everyone knew the Corner Sweet Shop, it was a landmark in the town and almost on the zebra crossing. Willie turned the door knob and a little bell inside gave a warning *ping*.

The Corner Sweet Shop lady was sitting by the telephone counting the money in the till. She knew Willie by sight as she knew all the boys and girls of the neighbourhood. She always gave them good measure for their money– and often a bit over.

"I was saving up for a silver whistle for when I'm a policeman," Willie told her, "but now I'm going to buy sweets instead."

"Well, just let me finish my accounts and then you can choose what you fancy. There's ice-cream left over today," she told him. "Go and wait in my room and we'll have that first –" and she went on counting "– fifty pence, one pound…"

Willie slipped behind the counter and through the little door that led into the Corner Sweet Shop lady's sitting-room. It was a bit dark but there was enough light coming in from the shop for Willie to see everything in the room: the little gas stove where a kettle was quietly singing to itself, a tray set with a tea-pot, a cup and saucer and a tin of biscuits, an armchair pulled up to a whispering fire. It was a cosy room smelling of toffee and chocolate and biscuits.

From the shop Willie could hear the Corner Sweet Shop lady murmuring over her figures. They were getting bigger now: "… five pounds ten pence, five pounds fifty."

The murmuring stopped and in a moment the Corner Sweet Shop lady came into the room. "Willie, will you mind the shop for me while I put the money into the Night Safe?" She went over to the fire and threw a log on to the glowing coals. "I'll hang the CLOSED card on the door and if the telephone rings, say I won't be a moment."

The Corner Sweet Shop lady had often left him minding the shop while she slipped down the road for this or that, and always she said: "If the telephone rings, answer it and say I won't be a moment" – but it never had. Willie went over to the counter and played with the telephone for a moment, moving the dial round to 999 because now there was no one to say 'Don't'. But, of course, he didn't lift the handpiece and so no one spoke back to him.

After that he wandered round the shop trying to make up his mind what he would buy. He could almost taste the delicious flavours as he read out the names. It seemed that he could almost smell them, too – except that the smell tickling his nose was not really a sweet smell but a smoky one. He looked up and saw that the shop was filled with a light grey haze. And now he could hear a soft crackling sound, not in the shop but coming from the sitting-room behind.

Willie ran round the back of the counter to where the door led into the sitting-room and behind the smoke he could see little dancing fingers of flame. He closed the door quickly. Perhaps if the door was shut the little flames would stay in the sitting-room. The Corner Sweet Shop lady had said to look after the shop for her but he was going to have to leave it to fetch help – and then his eye caught the telephone. He remembered the three words on the dial: Fire, Police, Ambulance, 999.

Whenever Willie had thought of using the telephone he had always thought of speaking to the Police, but now he realised they were only good for traffic jams and crimes: when you had a fire you needed a Fireman. He put a finger into the second hole at the bottom of the dial and this time he lifted the handpiece off its rest before he moved the dial round, three times – 999.

A voice answered him immediately: "What service do you want?"

The first time Willie opened his mouth he could not make any sound come, but the second time the word was there. "Fire," Willie said. There was a tiny pause and then a deep, slow, calm voice spoke: "High Street Fire Station. Will you give the correct address, please?"

"The Corner Sweet Shop – in the High Street." The man's voice was so quiet and calm that at once Willie felt quiet and calm, too.

"Will you repeat that address, please?" the voice said, "and give a cross reference."

Willie did not know what a cross reference was but it sounded as if the fireman wanted even more directions. "The Corner Sweet Shop in the High Street," Willie said again, and then remembered something else: "– near to the zebra crossing," he added. There was only one zebra crossing in the High Street, and everyone knew it was close to the Corner Sweet Shop. The man sounded satisfied and rang off and Willie put the handpiece back on its rest.

The door of the sitting-room was closed but little coils and whirls of smoke were puffing their way through the key-hole and round the edges of the door. Willie wasn't really frightened because he knew the firemen must already be on their way, but to be on the safe side he stood near the shop door ready to pop out into the High Street if he wanted to.

Through the Sweet Shop window he could see people hurrying by, quite unaware of what was happening in the little shop – and then above the rattle and rumble suddenly there was the wail of the fire-engine, and in a moment the great scarlet and silver monster was pulling up outside the shop, with blue lights flashing. Uniformed, helmeted men

came bursting out from it, and as they strode across the pavement. Willie opened the door.

Willie had never seen firemen quite so close before. They clattered into the shop, axes tucked into their belts, long water-proof leggings reaching up to their thighs, a long coiling hose snaking out behind them.

"Anyone on the premises?" one of the firemen asked Willie as the others pressed forward to the door behind the counter.

"No," Willie told him. "The Corner Sweet Shop lady had to go out. She asked me to mind the shop for her."

"Well, stand back out of the way," the fireman warned him. When they pushed open the sitting-room door Willie could hear the fire crackling and roaring and then spitting furiously as the stream of water from the hose struck into the centre of it.

Willie edged a little nearer but there were so many firemen in the little room and so much smoke and steam that he couldn't see the fire at all and then one of the firemen opened the window and the trapped smoke and steam poured out and drifted past the shop window and down the High Street.

"Don't tell me you started this little lot?"

Willie had not expected to see the policeman but suddenly he was there, the very one who had brought him home after his circus act. Willie was just opening his mouth to explain when in bustled the Corner Sweet Shop lady.

"Oh, my goodness me. And oh, Willie, you're safe and sound. Whatever happened?"

"I was in the shop deciding what to buy with my money," Willie told her, "and suddenly it was all smoky. I went to look in the sitting-room and the fire had come out on to the carpet."

"The log!" the Corner Sweet Shop lady exclaimed. "Oh dear, officer, it was all my doing. I threw it on before I went out."

"– and I suppose you didn't think to put the fire-guard in front of it before you left the room," the policeman said. "The usual story."

He reached for his note-book and pencil. "Who was it sent for the Brigade, then?" he asked. "They seem to have got here before too much damage was done."

"I did," Willie told him. "I dialled 999 and they came."

"And a lot less damage was done because the sitting-room door was closed," one of the firemen said, coming out of the room with a limp hose trailing behind him. "We didn't even have to fix up to a hydrant, there was enough water in the tank. I'd like to compliment someone on that."

"That must have been Willie, too," the Corner Sweet Shop lady said, "because I know I left it open."

"I closed it because I was afraid it would come out into the shop and burn up the chocolates and sweets," Willie explained. He had not known it was safer to keep doors and windows closed if there was a fire, but he'd make sure he remembered for another time.

"You're a natural, you are," the fireman said. "We could do with boys like you in the Brigade."

Willie was delighted. "Could you?" He looked at the firemen as they filed out of the shop. Their helmets were larger than policemen's helmets, and they wore axes in their belts instead of whistles in their pockets, and they rode on engines whereas all policemen had were motor-bikes and patrol cars.

"I wouldn't be surprised if there isn't a reward going for boys who have their heads screwed on the right way," the policeman said.

"A silver whistle, at least," the Corner Sweet Shop lady said. "And now, officer, could you take the boy home? His parents must be wondering what's happened to him."

Willie had forgotten all about it being nearly bedtime and that he was not supposed to go too far away. "I'll come and spend my money tomorrow," he told the Sweet Shop lady as the policeman hurried him through the waiting crowd outside the shop to the patrol car.

"Wherever have you been, Willie?" his mother scolded him. "It's past bedtime and I said not to go far away." She had had a harassing day, the baby troublesome, Willie not knowing what to do with himself, and Willie's father had come in tired and irritated and with some horrifying tale of a fire in the High Street and a traffic jam to end all traffic jams.

"I didn't go far," Willie said, "– only to the Corner Sweet Shop."

"But that's where the fire was," his father's voice was full of alarm.

"I know," Willie said, "I was there."

"You were there – ?" Willie's mother's voice was a squeak of fright.

"Nothing happened," Willie assured her. "I dialled 999 and the fire engines came."

His father opened his mouth but another voice spoke before he could:

"That's right, sir. You've got a smart son, sir." The officer had followed Willie into the sitting-room. "Very little damage was done due to the prompt action taken by your son. He won't make a policeman until he's grown a bit but he'd qualify any time for C.I.D., Special Branch."

"What's C.I.D., Special Branch?" Willie asked. He thought it sounded like some part of a tree.

"It's really another limb of the Law," the officer said. "Special Branch do the detective work and then we move in.

They don't need all those feet and inches and they don't need a uniform, they're just smart chaps with a lot of common sense."

Willie thought about it for a moment. It sounded all right, more important than being a policeman – but not really as important as a fireman.

"– and we'll see you get that whistle," the officer promised.

"I think, if you don't mind," Willie said, "I'd rather have an axe."

Fire-Brigade Willie

Willie was in the garden. It wasn't raining but the puddle of water he was standing in was as deep as if it had been. When he had turned on the tap he had not expected the water to run through the hose so quickly. It took him all his time to hang on to it, grasping the nozzle with both hands and pointing it the way he wanted the water to go. But one extra strong spurt turned the nozzle in his hands and the water went straight up the side of the house and in through the open kitchen window.

"Willie!" screamed his mother.

Willie hardly recognised her. The blast of water had caught her as she stood at the sink washing up the breakfast dishes: it had changed her nicely curled hair into strands of yellow wet seaweed.

"Look what you've done! – and I only had it set yesterday," his mother wailed.

"It wasn't meant to come up there," Willie explained. "The fire's in the basement."

"For heaven's sake – what fire?" In her alarm his mother forgot all about her spoiled hair-do and rushed out into the garden.

"It's only a pretend fire," Willie called reassuringly, but by this time his mother was there.

She turned off the tap and looked at Willie in despair.

"What am I to do with you?" she exclaimed. "Just look at the mess you're in. And the hose-pipe! Can't you leave anything alone?"

"How can I learn to be a fireman if I don't practise?" Willie wanted to know. It wasn't as big as the hose-pipe the firemen used but it worked almost as well, or at least it would have worked if he had been allowed to try it out properly.

"Now wind it back on its stand and go in and put some dry clothes on."

The hose continued to leak water as Willie wound it back on to its little wheel; it gave a final dribble and then dried up. Practising to be a fireman was more difficult than practising to be a policeman. You needed more clothes, too. For instance, if he'd had on real water-proof leggings and Wellington boots he wouldn't be having to take off his clothes and start dressing all over again.

"Being a fireman isn't playing with water all the time," Willie's father said when he came in. "There's a lot you have to know before you can be a fireman."

His father was right. Willie remembered the long ladder at the top of the fire-engine, and how it had a little platform on the end so that it could be run up the side of a high building when the firemen had to rescue people who had got trapped up there.

He went to look in the shed to see if the garden ladder was there. It wasn't often used: only in the springtime to trim back the creeper that grew on the wall of the house, and in the autumn to gather the apples from the trees. Of course it was a very light, short ladder and would not have been any use at all for rescuing people who were trapped at the top of a high building, but it would do to practise on.

He pulled it out of the shed – which was difficult because its legs were tangled up with a deck-chair and in freeing the deck-chair the ladder knocked against a tin of paint which had been put safely away on the top shelf. The tin went flying. It bounced on a shelf and came down on the handle of the lawn-mower. The bang loosened the lid so that it jumped off and splashed everything with red paint – including Willie.

"Willie!" His mother had heard the noise and came running from the house.

Now she hardly recognised Willie. His hair was streaked with bright red, there were blobs of it on his cheeks so that he looked like a circus clown, and it dripped from his fresh clean clothes.

"Oh, Willie – " She did not know whether to laugh or to cry.

"I was only getting the ladder out," Willie explained.

"You know the ladder isn't for you to play with."

"I wasn't going to play with it. I was going to rescue someone – "

"You're doing no rescuing of anyone," his mother told him, propping the ladder up against the shed and removing the now empty tin of red paint.

She cleaned Willie up with a rag dipped in turpentine. The touch of it made his skin tingle and the smell of it made his eyes smart. When it came to getting the paint out of his hair she had to clean each strand separately which took a long time and was very painful.

"Now go and have a bath," she told him, "– and don't let me see or hear from you until dinner-time."

There was a long time to go before it would be dinner-time. Willie walked round the garden – avoiding the shed – and came up to the garden gate. After he had dressed – for the third time that morning – he had put on his Wellington boots, although it was dry and the sun was shining, just in case. They didn't come as high up his legs as real firemen's boots would have done, but it was the best he could do.

The postman was coming down the road. He stopped when he saw Willie.

"What are we this morning?" he asked.

Willie knew what the postman meant. Once he had practised standing on his head so that he could be a turn in a circus, another time he had practised directing traffic so that he could be a policeman. Now he said: "I'm going to be a fireman."

The postman nodded understandingly. "I remember wanting to be a fireman," he said. A little picture flashed suddenly into his mind of himself, the same age as Willie was now, standing outside the fire-station, looking into the room where the engines were. As he stood there the alarm bell had begun to ring and from a hole in the ceiling above men came sliding down a pole, snatching at helmets, struggling into leggings and boots, piling on to the fire-engine as it swung out of the station, all the while fastening their

buttons and belts. "They all sit inside the fire-engine now –
like in a bus." he said. He was sorry about that. He didn't
think it was quite the same.

"What stopped you being a fireman?" Willie asked him.

"I don't know," the postman said. He hadn't thought about
it in years. "Maybe I wasn't smart enough. It takes learning
to be a fireman." He thought about it a bit now and then
said: "Don't get me wrong. It takes learning to be a postman,
too. And it's just as important." He straightened his
shoulders, bent under the weight of the mail sack. "On Her
Majesty's Service, delivering mail from all parts of the world.
Tell me anything more important than that?" He gave the
sack a little hitch and began to walk away; he'd wasted too
much time as it was. "Well, if I see a fire anywhere I'll let you
know."

The milkman came rattling round the corner and stopped
outside the gate. "Only three pints
today," he said, looking at the
little ticket Willie's mother
had tied round the neck of
one of the empty bottles.
"Who isn't drinking his pinta?"

"That was when I was going to be a policeman," Willie told him. "Now I'm going to be a fireman."

"Firemen need milk the same as policemen," the milkman said.

"But they don't have to be tall like policemen."

"Strong, though," the milkman said. "It isn't only fires they have to put out, you know."

"I know about the ladder," Willie said.

"Now, that's something, isn't it?" the milkman said. "Running a ladder up into the air, not standing it against anything – and a chap at the top playing his hose into a lot of flames and smoke." He shook his head. "It wouldn't do for me. I never could stand heights."

"What else do they do?" Willie asked him.

"Oh – rescue work," the milkman said.

"What kind of rescue work?" Willie wanted to know.

"You name it, they do it," the milkman said. "Why don't you go round and have a talk with them?"

Willie knew where the fire-station was, just down the road and a little way round the corner. He often heard the fire bell ringing but when he got to the gate the fire-engine had usually gone.

"A smart boy like you, they'd be glad to tell you anything."

"Do you think so?" Willie asked him.

"I'm sure so," the milkman said. "Well, I mean they've plenty of time to talk, there isn't a fire every day."

"I'll think about it," Willie said.

He thought about it until the milkman's trolley disappeared round the corner and then he set off.

Mrs Jones was coming out of Number 10. She was a friend of his mother's and taught at the big school at the end of the High Street. Now it was holidays and mostly she went away for the whole of them.

"As a matter of fact I'm off in a few moments," she told Willie, "but first I have to do last minute shopping."

Willie understood because that was the kind of shopping his mother often did.

"My bags are all packed and when I come back from the shops I go to catch my train."

They walked down the road together.

"Where are *you* going to?" she asked Willie.

"To the fire-station," Willie told her. "I'm going to be a fireman and the milkman said to go and talk to them."

"It takes a lot of courage to be a fireman," Mrs Jones said, and added as the milkman had: "It needs a head for heights too." Willie did not know if he had a head for heights or not, he'd never thought about it. He could stand on his head, but perhaps that was different.

"Well, I'll see you when I come back from my holidays," Mrs Jones said, "and then you must tell me all about it."

Willie walked on, round the corner and in the direction of the fire-station. He was nearly there when suddenly the alarm started ringing and out from the station a little ahead of him swung one fire-engine and then another: great scarlet, bus-like machines with neatly folded hosepipes and a ladder lying across the roof.

There hadn't been time to close the door at the back of the fire-engine and as it passed him Willie could see the firemen pulling on their water-proof leggings and thrusting their legs into high Wellington boots. Some had managed to get their helmets on and some hadn't, but you knew that by the time they got to the fire they would have everything in order and not a hair out of place. The alarm rang loudly and urgently and warningly and in a moment the fire-engine was out of sight. The traffic that had stopped now began to move again, and all the people on the street who had turned to stare went on their way once more.

Willie walked on to the fire-station although he thought it must be empty now, but there was one man left standing in the yard.

"Someone has to stay on duty," he told Willie, "– to answer the telephone, to send for reinforcements if necessary. On the other hand, that last call might be a false alarm and then they'll be back in two minutes flat. You haven't come to report another fire, I hope?"

"I want to be a fireman," Willie said. "The milkman said you'd tell me how."

"Well, now – it isn't as easy as all that," the fireman said. "First you have to grow, and then there's school, and after that there's special learning."

Being a fireman sounded a long way off. "What about –

rescue work ?" Willie asked him.

"All part of it," the fireman said. "You can't have one without the other."

"But what do you rescue?"

"Dogs that have fallen down wells, cats that have got caught up trees and daren't come down, folks who get trapped – inside or outside of places. You'd be surprised what tricks sensible human beings and animals get up to."

"And that's when you use the ladder?" Willie said.

"That's right, the ladder and a bit of common sense. Don't let me put you off, though. We're always wanting new recruits. Come back when you're a bit older."

Willie walked slowly back down the High Street and turned the corner into his own road. Whatever he wanted to be, the answer was always the same: he wasn't old enough, or tall enough, or strong enough.

"Willie! Willie!"

He turned round and it was Mrs Jones, standing at her gate waving at him excitedly. He walked the few steps back to Number 10.

"Oh, Willie – I'm in such trouble. I've locked myself out and only half an hour before my train goes."

Willie looked up at the house. It was exactly the same as the one he lived in just down the road. The curtains were drawn and the windows were tightly closed except for one small one on the first floor.

"I haven't a ladder," Mrs Jones said, "and if I had I couldn't get through that little space."

"I could," Willie said.

"Oh, but it's too dangerous," Mrs Jones protested. "I was thinking you might run for the fire-brigade for me."

"They've all gone to a fire," Willie told her, "– all except one and he's on duty."

"Oh dear, oh dear, what will I do? Perhaps if I knocked next door –" Mrs Jones began.

"We've got a ladder," Willie said quickly. It didn't have to be a very long one because Mrs Jones's window wasn't very high up. "I'll fetch it," he told her, and ran off down the street before she could open her mouth to stop him.

The ladder was outside the shed where his mother had left it. It wasn't very heavy. Willie took hold of it by the last rung and pulled it after him – down the path, through the gate, and into the street. Mrs Jones's house was only two or three doors away and when she saw him she came out to help him.

"Are you sure you can do it, Willie?" she asked anxiously. To be quite honest, the man next door would not have done at all because he was fat and would never have been able to squeeze through the small window, but Willie was just the right size. "I'll hold it firmly at the bottom and if it begins to feel too high for you to climb, you must come down."

Willie went up the ladder quickly. Mrs Jones looked quite different from above: short and squat, and with a balding little patch on the top of her head that you never would have seen looking up at her.

"I'm nearly there," he called down. It really was higher than he had ever been before, much higher than any of the trees he was used to climbing, but in a moment he was up against the window. As a matter of fact, Willie at first

thought there was someone inside looking out at him but then he realised it was his own reflection gazing back at him.

He lifted a hand from the ladder and, feeling through the little open space, found the arm that held the window open and unhooked it from the staple. It was a good thing, Willie thought, that Mrs Jones's house was the same as his own or he might not have been able to manage so easily. He pushed the window open as wide as it would go and then threw one leg over the ledge.

He had expected the room he looked into to be the same, too, but it was lined with shelves all filled with books, and what his feet touched as he reached down was a desk.

He looked around him for a moment and then jumped

down, careful not to disturb anything – the typewriter, a tape-recorder, and the books that overflowed the shelves and were piled everywhere. There were so many books that there could not be anything Mrs Jones did not know everything about: how to be a policeman, how to be a detective, how to be a fireman. Willie would have liked to stop and look inside some of them but he remembered just in time that Mrs Jones was waiting to be let in – and she had a train to catch.

He ran down the stairs to the front door. He had to stand on tip-toe to reach the door lock, but he was used to that and he knew he could do it.

"Oh, Willie – I don't know how to thank you," Mrs Jones

said. "There isn't time to reward you now, but I will when I get back. You think of something you really want and I'll see what I can do." She picked up the suitcases that were sitting just inside the front door.

"There isn't time, either, to help you with the ladder. Leave it where it is and your father will carry it back."

Willie was sure firemen did not fetch their fathers to help carry their ladders, so as soon as Mrs Jones had disappeared down the road, he picked it up by the bottom rung again and dragged it through the gate and back the short distance to his own home.

Willie's mother was just coming out into the garden to

hang clothes on the line when Willie came through the gate pulling the ladder behind him.

"Willie – what did I tell you about leaving that ladder alone? Where have you been with it?"

"I've been doing rescue work," Willie told her.

"Rescue work?" Willie's mother did not have any other words left.

"Mrs Jones was locked out and her luggage was locked in.

She was going to call the fire-brigade – but they'd all gone out to a fire. If I hadn't rescued her she would have missed her train."

"You mean – you climbed in – through a window?"

Willie nodded. His mother was looking astonished and alarmed – but not angry any more.

"Mrs Jones held the ladder. It was quite safe." It had been a bit frightening, too, but he wasn't going to say that.

"What *am* I to do with you, Willie? You'll probably make a wonderful fireman when you grow up, but in the meantime you can't go practising all over the place."

"I'm not going to be a fireman any more." Willie dragged the ladder over to the garden shed and laid it down.

"Oh – so what is it now?" Willie's mother did not know whether to be relieved or worried all over again. What Willie wanted to be now might be even worse than being a policeman, or a special branch detective, or a fireman –

"Mrs Jones said I was to think of something I wanted as a reward."

"Oh –" his mother said again. She waited. She could not begin to imagine what it was going to be this time.

"There's a lot you have to know before you can be a fireman," Willie said, repeating what his father had said and what the milkman and the officer on duty at the fire-station had said. "It isn't as easy as all that. You have to have – learning. With learning you can be anything."

"Oh –" his mother said. There was really nothing else to say.

"Mrs Jones's house is full of books and they're full of the things you have to know before you can be anything. If I go to her school she'll teach me."

"School!" Willie's mother had been counting the months

and the weeks and the days to the time Willie would be able to go to school, and wondering how they were going to persuade him to go – and here he was, asking to.

"I think – for my reward," Willie said, "I'll have a school-bag."